THE ITCH IN MY ITCH PANTS

Krystaelynne Sanders
Illustrated by Thais Libório

This Book Belongs To:

_____

A tickling crazy itch crawls inside my pants.

It starts with a tingle and makes me want to dance.

I can't focus on anything.
It's ruining my day.

My mom says it may
need to be cleaned.

I shower and wash
all areas in between.

But later,
the itch starts to appear.

Oh, I want to scratch it
and make it disappear.

I go to my dad and
ask for some help.
He sees me squirming and
lets out a yelp.

"What's wrong, my dear child?"
he asks with a smile,
"Is it the itch that's
been driving you wild?"

I nod my head and give a little whine. "It's so itchy, I can't get it out of my mind."

Dad says, "I think I know what's causing your itch. You need to wipe after you've finished your business!"

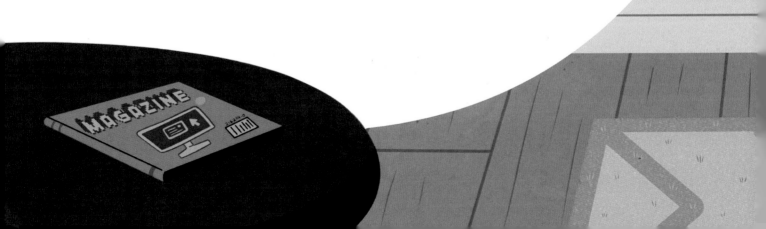

I hang my head and
admit I forgot.

I was in a hurry and
just gave it a shot.

Dad says, "No worries,
we'll fix this right up.

Wiping properly is easy.
Let's get you cleaned up."

"First grab some toilet paper, the size of your palm,

wipe from front to back...

...until you feel clean and calm."

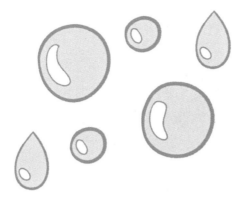

Next, he reminds me to
wash my hands well.
To keep them clean and
free from any smell.

I follow his instructions
and soon feel relieved.
The itch is gone,
and I'm finally free!

Learning to wipe can
be tough at the start,

But wiping right
will soothe that itchy part.

So when you feel the itch down below,
Remember to wipe, and the itch will go.

About the Author

Krystaelynne is an author dedicated to using her writing to educate and empower children. With a background in criminal justice, political science, and ethnic studies, she has made it her mission to prevent child sexual abuse and promote positive self-esteem in young readers. As a mother, Krystaelynne is passionate about providing children with the tools they need to develop confidence and strength in facing life's challenges. In her work as an advocate, she is committed to positively impacting children's lives. Krystaelynne currently resides in Northern California with her husband and son, who provide her with love and support in her work as an advocate.

In addition to her books, Krystaelynne offers bulk discounts, school visits, and more. To learn more and stay updated, visit her website and follow her on social media.

Website: ksdiggs.com
Email: author@ksdiggs.com
Instagram: @allthingsdiggs
Facebook: Author K Sanders Diggs

Scan for Important Links >>>